Amy's Wonderful Nest

WITHDRAWN

GORDON SNELL
• Pictures by Fergus Lyons •

THE O'BRIEN PRESS
DUBLIN

First published 1997 by The O'Brien Press Ltd,
12 Terenure Road East, Rathgar, Dublin 6, Ireland.
Tel: +353 1 4923333; Fax: +353 1 4922777
E-mail: books@obrien.ie
Website: www.obrien.ie
Reprinted 1999, 2000, 2003, 2006.

ISBN-10: 0-86278-530-8
ISBN-13: 978-0-86278-530-7

British Library Cataloguing-in-Publication Data
Snell, Gordon
Amy's wonderful nest. - (O'Brien pandas)
1.Children's stories
I.Title
II.Lyons, Fergus
823.9'14[J]

5   6   7   8   9   10
06   07   08   09   10

The O'Brien Press receives
assistance from

the arts
council
schomhairle
ealaíon

Typesetting, layout, editing and design: The O'Brien Press Ltd
Printing: Cox & Wyman Ltd

Can YOU spot the panda
hidden in the story?

Amy was a baby robin.
She lived in a warm nest
with her mother and father
and her sisters and brothers.

The nest was high up in a tree,
safe from cats and dogs.

The little robins could not
fly yet. So every day their
mother and father
flew away to find food for them.
They told Amy and the others
to stay at home inside the nest.

Amy wished she could fly.
She watched her mother and
father, then she flapped
her wings like they did,
but nothing happened.

She looked out over
the edge of the nest
at the big world outside.

Amy wished she could see
more. She stood on the edge
of the nest and looked over.
It was a very long way
down to the ground.

Amy leaned over ... and over ...

And she fell!

Down, down she went, until

BUMP

she hit the ground.

She lay gasping on the grass.

She looked up at the tree
where the nest was.
How would she ever
get home again?
Poor Amy felt all alone.
She did not know what to do.

Soon she stood up and
began to hop around.
She came to a field.
There was a gate there,
and it was open.

Then Amy heard loud snorts
and tramping feet.
A herd of cows was coming
through the gate!

Tramp! Tramp! they went. 'Oh no!' said Amy. 'What will I do?' She hid in the grass, shaking.

The huge feet stamped around
her. Amy waited for a foot
to stand on her, but luckily
they all missed.

'I must build a **nest**,' Amy
said. 'Then I'll be safe.'
There was a wall nearby.
Some of the stones had fallen
down and Amy scrambled
up to the top of the wall.

'I'll be safe here,' she said.
'I'll make my nest here.'

Then Amy stopped
and thought.

What was a nest made of?
She could not remember.

And how is a nest built?
She did not know.
She had never seen one
being built before.

'Oh dear,' said Amy, 'I'll just have to work it out for myself. I'll look around for things I can use.'

She climbed down the stones
and hopped to a nearby
farmyard. The very first thing
she saw there was ...

... a broken old box.
It was a bit messy,
but Amy did not mind.
She pulled it up to the top
of the stones.

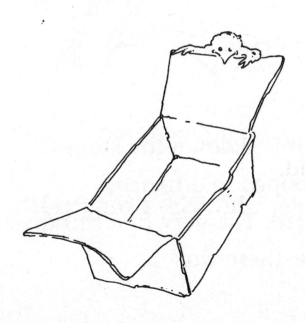

'Now, that's a great start,'
she said.
'I wonder what else I can find?'

She found a wrapper
from a chocolate bar.
It was bright and shiny.
She picked it up in her beak,
but it stuck to her.
She pulled it off with her foot,
and it stuck to her foot!

'Oh no!' Amy said, 'this is
a lot of trouble!'
In the end she got it to
the top of the stones.
She stuck it on the box.
'That makes a nice picture,'
she said.
Then she set off again.

Next she found
a round beer mat.
It was very smelly,
but Amy picked it up.
'Yuck!' she said.

She tried to hold her breath
as she pulled it up the stones.
'I'll put it outside the nest,'
she said. 'It will put off
burglars!'

WITHDRAWN

Then she found a crumpled
page from a comic.
She picked it up and it blew
over her face.
She could not see a thing.
She stumbled and fell over.

After a long time she got it
to the nest.
'That makes a nice carpet,'
she said. 'Now, what else
can I find?'

She found a banana skin.
It was very slippery.

At the top of the stones
Amy fell on the skin
and slid down!
'I'll put this at the door,'
she said, 'then I can slide
out of my nest!'

Next she found
a baby's woolly hat.
It was old and torn, but Amy
said, 'That's nice and fluffy.
It will make a lovely
warm bed for me.'

She put it in a corner of the nest
and curled up on it to try it out.
It was soft and warm
and cuddly.

Then some leaves fell down on
top of her head.
'I can use these too,' she said.
She put them around
the sides of the nest.

'My nest is still not finished,'
Amy said. She went out to find
more things. You'll never guess
what she found ...

A big long feather.
It tickled her beak and
made her giggle.

Amy stuck it up in the middle
of the nest. 'It will wave in the
wind like a flag,' she said.
'And I'll always be able to
find my way home.
Now, what else can I get?'

She saw a pink fluffy thing.
Amy did not know what it was,
but it was a powder puff.
'This is nice and soft,'
she said. 'It would make
a good pillow.' She picked it up
and sneezed.

'Aaaaa-choooo.'

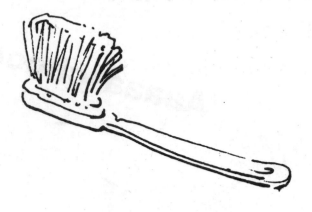

An old toothbrush was next.
'Great!' said Amy. 'I can use it
to brush my feathers.'

She put it in a corner
of the nest.
And what did she find then?

An empty ice-cream tub.
'When it rains, this will make a
splendid bath!' said Amy.

Now the nest was getting
a bit wobbly and
Amy needed something
to hold it together.

And what do you think
she found?

A long piece of ribbon.
She tied it all around the nest,
and put a big bow in front.

Amy's nest was finished!

Amy looked proudly at her nest.
'That's a great nest,' she said.
'But I'm tired from finding
all those things.'
She got into her nest
and lay down on the bed.
Soon she was asleep.

While she slept someone came
and lifted up the nest
with Amy inside on to
a high branch of a tree.
When Amy woke up
her nest was in
a different place!

But it was much safer up here,
away from cats and dogs.

Then she heard a voice.
'Wow! This nest is just the best!'
it said. It was a sparrow.
He flew off to tell all his friends
about the wonderful nest.
Soon lots of birds were at the
tree.

An old owl arrived.
'I am the judge of the
Nest of the Year competition,'
she said.
'And this nest is the best.
Amy, you get First Prize.'

She gave Amy a huge rosette
and a banner that said

BEST

NEST

OF

THE

YEAR.

All the birds cheered.

Then came the best surprise.
Amy's mother and father
flew over to see the
winning nest.
'Amy!' they said. **'We've
found you at last!.'**

Amy hopped up and down
with excitement.
'Can we go home now?'
she said.
'Home?' said her mother.
'No! You made such
a wonderful nest, Amy,
that we'll all come
and live here instead.'

And so Amy's whole family
came to live in
Amy's Wonderful Nest.

Well, did you find him?